The Wonderful Once

A Christmas Story

By

J. R. Buchta

Illustrations by Erin O'Leary Brown

Library of Congress Control Number: 2023902117

ISBN 979-8-9869895-0-1 (Paperback)
ISBN 979-8-9869895-2-5 (Hardcover)
ISBN 979-8-9869895-3-2 (Hardcover with Dust Jacket)
ISBN 979-8-9869895-1-8 (Ebook)

JUVENILE FICTION/Holidays & Celebrations/Christmas & Advent

Illustrations and cover art by Erin O'Leary Brown at www.eobrownart.com
Interior and cover design by Michelle M. White at mmwbooks.com

For more information, visit
www.thewonderfulonce.com/

For permissions and bulk book orders, contact
emily@thewonderfulonce.com

Yardley, Pennsylvania, USA

Kindness is the most powerful magic known . . .

It beats truest in the hearts of children.

For my child, Emily and her children, Mackie, Cooper, and Leo.

JRB

Most things in life happen over and over again.
Some things happen only once.
This is the story of a wonderful once.

It all began in a small village nestled in a peaceful valley. Friendly people filled happy hours and carefree children ran and played through the narrow streets. A dressmaker, a carpenter, a baker, a blacksmith, and a shopkeeper made the village square a busy hub of goings on and a fine place for gatherings and conversation. The surrounding farms were green in summer and perfect for sledding in winter.

In the middle of the village, a special school cared for boys and girls who didn't have a home. The devoted headmaster and teachers treated the children well. Most children spent only a brief time at the school before loving parents adopted them.

The best time of year at the school was just after the harvest, around the time of the first snowfall. The village came alive with activity as everyone prepared for the annual winter festival. Villagers decorated their houses and businesses with colorful ribbons and evergreens. Warm kitchens glowed with fires and the mouthwatering aroma of cakes and pies filled the air.

Each year, villagers donated everything necessary for the school's celebration. The dressmaker, carpenter, and blacksmith made toys for all the children. The townsfolk prepared a great feast, including a mountain of desserts.

The children looked forward to the festival with delicious anticipation. As they ate, the boys and girls eyed the gifts piled in the corner of the room, hoping to be the first to select a present from the tower of mysterious delights.

Before dessert, each child chose a gift.

At one particular festival, Lucas, the youngest child, went first. Feeling a bit shy, he took his time approaching the pile of treasures. As he drew near, his shyness turned to excitement.

Which one to choose?

Big or small? Heavy or light?

Not wanting to seem selfish or unkind, he chose the smallest gift.

He tingled as he unwrapped it. What was it? When he untied the ribbon and peeled back the cloth, a beautiful, hand-carved sleigh appeared. It was fine in every detail—made by hands that loved the wood and painted by an artist who chose the brightest red, the blackest black, and the shiniest gold.

Full of joy, Lucas smiled. Perfection. He had never been happier in his life. He couldn't take his eyes off the sleigh as he traced its borders with his fingers and gave the tiny bells a jingle.

As the night went on, each child selected a gift from the pile until none were left.

The party continued with more food, laughter, music, and well-told stories to amuse the children. One teacher juggled, and another performed magic tricks. Everyone was filled with a festive spirit that gave the room a life that lit all their faces. What could be better?

As the hour grew late, they heard a knock at the door of the school. The headmaster opened it to a tall man and a little girl. They brushed the snow from their clothes and entered. Everyone could see that the little girl was sad.

The tall man explained to the headmaster that the little girl didn't have a home and needed to stay at the school until a family adopted her. This was the most difficult time for any child new to the school. She felt alone and wondered what would happen next.

Everyone tried to make her feel welcome, but all the merriment in the room didn't change how she felt. Watching her, Lucas felt sad, too.

With only one toy for each child, the new girl would be without one. At that moment, Lucas had an idea…he would give the little girl his toy…the sleigh.

Lucas held the sleigh in both hands as he approached the table where she sat. With outstretched arms, he presented the sleigh to her.

"For you," said Lucas.

The look of disbelief on her face soon became a bright smile.

"Thank you," she whispered.

That was it! The wonderful once.

That was the moment that changed Lucas forever.

He experienced a feeling unlike any other. Sure, he had felt wonderfully happy when he received his sleigh, but this was something entirely different. He wished that he could hold onto this feeling forever. He realized that giving a gift was far better than getting one.

Nothing in Lucas' short life had prepared him
for what would happen next.

At first, his happiness made it hard to fall asleep, but soon enough a cloud of drowsiness carried him off to Dreamland. He floated above Dreamland like a feather, enjoying the pleasure that comes from knowing that all is well, and that he had done his best.

The best part of his dream came in a sleepy vision. He saw a woman dressed in a flowing robe of red velvet tied with a white and silver ribbon. Her long hair fell over her shoulders like a golden waterfall.

In a word, she was beautiful … and not just in appearance. She projected a calming aura of peace and friendliness that put Lucas at ease.

"I believe introductions are in order," said the woman.

"I'm Lucas, Lucas Astan," he said.

"I am the Spirit of Giving," she said with a smile that warmed Lucas.

"Oh," said Lucas, "pleased to meet you."

"I'm the one who's pleased," said the Spirit. "I saw how generous and kind you were to the new girl, and how you unselfishly gave away your precious sleigh to make her feel welcome."

"How did you know about that?" asked Lucas.

"Wherever and whenever a good turn is done, I'm there," answered the Spirit.

"I felt happy giving away my toy," said Lucas. "I wish I could give every girl and boy in the world a toy."

"Hmmm," said the Spirit of Giving, "that sounds like a great idea. How can we make it happen?"

"I don't know," replied Lucas.

The Spirit thought for a moment before she spoke, "I think I can help make your dream come true."

She told Lucas that she would return the next morning and adopt him. That would be the first step to following his dream.

As promised, she returned and pledged to take care of Lucas forever. They said their goodbyes to the headmaster, teachers, and children, leaving the new little girl for last.

They hugged each other without saying a word. Instead, they exchanged grateful looks that made them both happy.

As Lucas and the Spirit walked away down the village street, they began making plans.

"I know a place where we can make your dream come true," the Spirit said. "It's a bit chilly, but we'll have all the help and magic we need."

She took Lucas by the hand and said,

"Close your eyes, Lucas, and think a happy thought."

And just like that,

they floated away

and landed in

the softest

snow

imaginable.

"Where are we?" asked Lucas, looking around in amazement.

The Spirit whispered in his ear, "It's the North Pole."

"It really is cold here," said Lucas through chattering teeth.

"I can help with that," said the Spirit.

With a wave of her hand and a nod of her head,
she magically wrapped the boy in a suit of red velvet.

"That's much better," sighed Lucas.

They walked over a beautiful snow drift and there, in all its charm and beauty, sat a tiny, magical village. As they approached, Lucas saw some of its residents.

"Who are they?" he asked the Spirit.

"They're Elves," she replied, "and they will help us make the toys. The Elves have been making toys for themselves for years and they're exceptionally good at it."

"How did they get here?" asked Lucas.

"Many years ago, during a very big storm, stardust and snowflakes swirled together to create the Elves," she explained, "It was magic."

As they walked through the village, the Spirit introduced Lucas to the Elves. As everyone knows, Elves have a knack for knowing who's naughty and who's nice. They quickly saw Lucas as among the nicest of them all.

"This is all so fantastic," exclaimed Lucas, "But after we make all the toys, how will I deliver them to the children?"

"Ahh," said the Spirit with a smile, "Follow me."

She led Lucas to a large red barn. They stopped before entering and the Spirit asked Lucas to close his eyes again.

"Are we going on another trip?" asked Lucas.

"No," said the Spirit patiently, "just close your eyes."

When he opened his eyes, he saw it! An exact replica of the sleigh he had given to the new girl at the school . . . only this time it was full sized and hitched up to a team of reindeer.

"Oh my," said Lucas smiling.

It was perfection.

Lucas' heart beat fast. He felt thrilled.

25

"Are the reindeer strong enough to pull a sleigh full of toys?" Lucas wondered aloud.

"Get in," encouraged the Spirit, "Let's see."

Lucas jumped into the sleigh and gave the reins a gentle tug. With that, the sleigh moved forward and upward!

"Wow!" shouted Lucas. "They can fly!"

The Spirit smiled.

"Stardust and snowflakes are a very powerful combination," she said.

Lucas guided the flying sleigh back down to the ground amid a chorus of jingling bells and swirling snow.

As he climbed out, he asked the Spirit of Giving, "But, when? When should I deliver the toys?"

"How about Christmastime?" suggested the Spirit.
Lucas nodded his head in agreement.

"Yes," he replied, "that would
be wonderful."

"Now that our plan is complete, we have only one detail left. What shall we call you?" asked the Spirit.

"What's wrong with Lucas?" he asked.

"Nothing," she said, "Lucas is a fine name, but let's make it a name that children around the world will remember."

They walked over to a workbench where an elf was making building blocks with letters of the alphabet painted on them.

"Hmmm," said the Spirit, "Let's see. Your name is Lucas Astan."

She spelled it very slowly as one by one she selected blocks with the same letters.

"L-U-C-A-S A-S-T-A-N"

She placed each block in a velvet sack and shook them. When she spilled the blocks onto the workbench, they spelled

"SANTA CLAUS"

"That's you," said the Spirit, "You are Santa Claus."

That was it! The plan was complete. The Wonderful Once had worked its magic and Lucas' dream had come true.

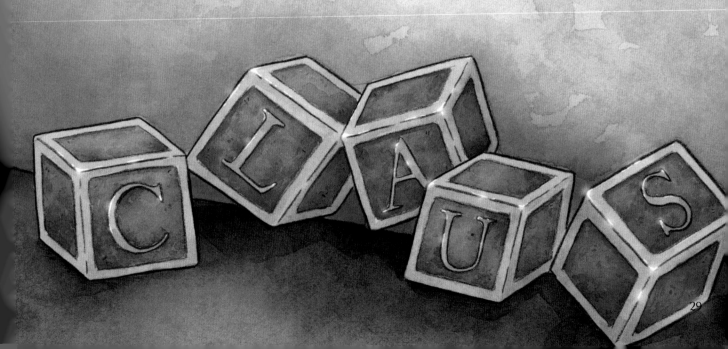

And so it was, from that day forward, he was Santa.

Over the years he became plump and grew a beautiful white beard.

But mostly he grew to appreciate his good fortune at being able to make other boys and girls happy ... and how the power of a single unselfish gesture changed the world forever.

WITH GRATITUDE

For Tea, Sympathy, and Hard Work: Melissa Warner and Emily Buchta.

For her beautiful illustrations: Erin O'Leary Brown.
I remain your biggest fan!

My sisters, Pat and Alma: I am grateful … they know why.

My father: for the inspiration.

A variety of talents helped make this book a reality. I am grateful to
Diana Needham and Karen Warner Schueler for their guidance,
Julie Cullen for her fine editing, and
Michelle M. White for the layout and design.

ABOUT THE AUTHOR

John Buchta was born and raised in Philadelphia, PA.

As a youngster he expressed an interest in music and spent most of his early life in the performing arts as a singer-songwriter. After graduating from the University of Pennsylvania, he entered the business world and made a career in marketing for various entrepreneurial ventures.

His interest in writing took a turn towards children's books when his grandchildren were born, and he recognized the power of their imaginations and their enjoyment of reading. His writing is inspired by memories of his childhood and the spirit of his father's character and penchant for a good story or poem.

Today, he resides in Bucks County PA with his wife.

ABOUT THE ILLUSTRATOR

Erin O'Leary Brown is an illustrator based in upstate NY, specializing in children's illustration as well as botanical and nature themes. She works traditionally in watercolor, and often utilizes digital media to adjust the final illustrations.

Over the years, Erin has worked in freelance illustration creating art for various books and children's magazines, as well as decorative designs, for clients such as Llewellyn Worldwide, Cricket Media and Scholastic.

She received a BFA in Illustration from Syracuse University, and an MS in Education from Elmira College. In addition to working in the field of illustration, she has also spent some time teaching art. More of Erin's work can be seen on her website at eobrownart.com.

Made in United States
Orlando, FL
24 November 2023

39356754R00024